TO,

My dear frier

Invisible Sun

With Love,

Jean x

Invisible Sun

Stories by

Jan Hunter

First published 2015
by Mudfog Press
c/o Arts and Events, Culture and Tourism,
P.O. Box 99A, Civic Centre, Middlesbrough, TS1 2QQ
www.mudfog.co.uk

Cover Design by turnbull.fineart@btinternet.com

Print by Evoprint & Design Ltd.

ISBN: 978-1-899503-96-4

Mudfog Press gratefully acknowledges
the support of Arts Council England.

Contents

Unconditional Love

Memories come in scraps and shades, some bright and clear, others misty and unsure. As a child my dreams were vivid. Which ones were my reality?

Petunias in bright masses, cascading along the mossy path. Ivy, and dappled sunlight, warm smells of pastry, of succulent gravy, never tasted since.

The village. My nurse's uniform, tending to the postman and to imaginary patients. Sitting on the counter in my father's butcher's shop, listening to the laughter and the banter. Avoiding the huge walk-in fridge which scared me, looking into the soulless eyes of the dead animals. Watching big men in their bloody white coats, scrubbing deeply grooved wooden counters and chopping boards.

Laughing, always laughter. I was brought up on laughter, despite my grandfather's suicide and the carefulness of those early post-war years.

The farm, the idyllic years. Little, yellow chicks in the kitchen, wobbly and innocent like me. Eagerly sucking lambs and calves, keeping warm by the jet black Aga, which smelt of doughy bread. The evil farm assistant whom we hated, with his crinkled eyes and nut-brown face. He drowned little kittens in a grey steel bucket, and had a one-eyed dog who growled at us when we collected the milk from the cowshed. He was our nightmare, along with the hissing geese who flapped at us when we took warm cans of tea to the men working on the threshing machine. We were too afraid to return to the safety of the farm, as the cows barred our way, staring at us with their sad eyes, silently moving their sideways mouths in unison.

Burniston Rocks. Endless holidays filled with sunshine. Following Aunty Lydia down the long lane. Buckets full of crabs and winkles, sandy socks and salty shins, and the long walk home.

Scary nightmares about the war. Stories from Bob, my father. Curling up tight in bed and worrying. Would it happen again? Thunderstorms, and dreams of lions with big teeth. The reassuring reflection of the paraffin lamp on the ceiling in my parent's bedroom.

But above all, boundless unconditional love, filling every crack of wherever we lived or whatever we did. Never judging, always loving, trusting and giving. That was my mother. And that was how we thought it would always be, and through the turmoil of those university years, through marriage, divorce and our father's too early death, this love sustained us.

It began slowly at first, the intrusion of this unwelcome stranger who would not leave. It was something that could not be ignored or laughed about. It was here to stay. Forgetfulness.

But I am like that too. Too much to think about. Too many roles in my life to fulfill. Mum sent my husband a, "Happy Birthday, Grandson" card. We laughed. She laughed too. The grandchildren she adored. Their birthdays passed her by. When she came to stay we would hear her in the night, restless, pacing, endlessly searching through her things. What was she searching for?

We arranged to meet her at York Station. We would have a family day out. She wasn't there. Frantically searching, searching, the tannoy booming out her name. My children turned to me with startled eyes, questioning, 'Where's Nana?' Meeting her by chance outside the station. 'How nice to see you, dear.' She looked bemused by our worried faces. My elegant and beautiful mother in a stained dress and shredded tights.

Trips across the moors to visit. My independent mother in sheltered accommodation. The warden had a pinched, grey face, devoid of understanding. 'Your mother must keep her flat clean. She breaks things. She is untidy. I complain to her frequently.'

The dust, the rotting food, the uneaten scraps. I cleaned and cleaned, my tears mingling with the soap and grime. What was happening to my mum?

I bought her a diary. I marked her appointments, underlining them in red ink. Her bills piled up in dusty corners. I took her shopping. I made her eat. My sweet, bewildered children helping to dust and clean, found two thousand pounds amongst her once treasured things.

We laughed with her. Nana was eccentric and funny. She danced in the street and she sang loudly in restaurants. She lifted her skirts and displayed her underwear in shops. She dared do things that were not allowed.

We bought her new clothes, my once slim mother was putting on weight. We hung on to her in case she escaped from the fitting rooms.

I peeled off two dresses, four vests and a nightie. She would run outside the changing rooms in her underwear shouting and swearing. Nana was so funny.

The last time we took her out for a meal was on her birthday in May. The woods were filled with the heavy scent of bluebells. The light was golden with a hint of warmer days to come. The streets of Scarborough were still quiet; the locals were preparing for the summer rush of visitors. We still call this place, Nana's cafe. She loved it here. It was where she and her friends would meet to share memories and family news. We collected her from her little flat, and we trooped into the cafe, our arms full of flowers and presents.

Everything was going well at first. Mum looked lovely in her three sets of beads and re-buttoning her clothes was not a problem. She was so pleased to see us. During the course of the meal she began to get restless and she began to raise her skirts, declaring that she was uncomfortable. My daughter and I kept reassuring her, gently making her decent again by pulling down her skirts underneath the table, without anyone noticing.

We got through the first course without much trouble, explaining to my curious son that Nana liked sugar in her soup, and that was the way it was. However, she gradually became more and more agitated, and without further ado she promptly pulled out her chair and lifted her leg onto the table, displaying an assortment of underwear, determined to show us all exactly where she was feeling uncomfortable.

The children disappeared under the table to pick up the items which had been swept aside by this unexpected event. I scrutinised the offending leg, as if this was the most natural thing in the world to happen. Ignoring any interested parties, I managed to persuade her to lower her leg as the roast lunch arrived.

We all tucked in, pretending that nothing unusual had happened, when suddenly my ladylike Mother threw her knife and fork onto the table with a resounding bang. 'I'm not eating this!' announced this elegant lady who wore matching hats, shoes and bags and who insisted that we always speak quietly in restaurants, 'It's shit!'

Time stood still momentarily in the cafe. The clatter of cutlery ceased, exchanged pleasantries were hushed. Our family was fixed in a small and silent tableau, forks poised to our mouths. I stood up quickly and then bounded over to the till, whilst the children bundled my indignant Mother (who had never to my knowledge uttered a swear word in her life) out onto the street, with the speed of a silent movie.

I closed the door of the cafe with as much dignity as I could muster, and turned to face my two wide-eyed children who were looking for an explanation. My mother stood between them, her arms holding them close, with mashed potato dripping down her cardigan, and the menu held firmly in a tight fist.

We looked from one to the other in awkward silence until my son declared, 'Nana said our dinner was shit.'

'Well it was,' I replied quickly and we started to giggle.

We wandered down to the beach together, still helpless with laughter, Mum joining in, wiping her eyes on one of her many underskirts.

'Do you want to see me dance?' she asked, her eyes sparkling as she kicked off her shoes into the sand.

'Well, why not?' I said, clasping her bird-like hands, as the children ran, squawking with embarrassment, down to the sea.

Two months later we got a call from a neighbour. My mother couldn't find her way home. She had forgotten where she lived. She was found wandering the streets in her night clothes. Frantic phone calls to my sisters, advice from her doctor, my doctor, a specialist. We have to put her in a home.

She barricaded herself in the bathroom, like she did when we tried to organise meals on wheels, home help, social services. She cried and cried. We heard her sobbing from the other side of the door. 'How can you do this to me?'

The terrible unspeakable guilt.

'You will break up your family if she lives with you,' advised my doctor. 'She needs specialist care 24/7.'

'But she's my mother. We promised never to put her in a home.'

My younger sister arrived from Canada, the shock showing plainly on her face. We had to do it but we didn't know how. We would have to lie.

'We are taking you to a hotel, Mum, for a little break.'
Her eyes lit up. She always loved to travel.

'With you three? It's ages since we all went away together.'

She clapped her hands together with excitement. She wanted us to take her shopping, to buy new clothes for the trip.

'I think I'd like a little job,' she smiled, 'as soon as we get back.'

'Well they may need someone to help in the hotel, Mum, you could stay there.' My younger

sister glanced at me. I looked away feeling like Judas.

The warden of the sheltered accommodation looked at us with steel, grey eyes when we informed her of our plans.

'What cruel children you are.'

She sniffed at us in disbelief, as we handed her weeks of unpaid rent.

'Make sure that you clean the place before you leave, and don't take any light fittings.'

We toured the homes. We saw the results of Alzheimers. We stared out along Scarborough beach where we had played as children and we cried.

We arrived to take Mum away and there was a party. Relatives and residents sat around tables with starched, white cloths, eating strawberry scones.

'Look, everyone!' My mother in her blue and white dress with all the buttons done up wrongly, ran towards us smiling. 'My lovely daughters.'

The warden with the cold eyes stared at us as we took her away. I drove, my hands were shaking. My sisters, hands holding mother tightly, talked incessantly. Her hands, now so claw-like, gripped our clothes,

'But aren't you coming too?'

We drove off. We left her there with her little case, surrounded by her once treasured possessions, a bewildered look on her face, her hands plucking at her skirt. My elder sister left to go back to Leeds. There was nothing else to say.

'I need a drink.' My younger sister broke the silence. We sat in a bar that overlooked the sea. The train trickled down the windows. We couldn't find anything to say to each other. There were no words to describe how we felt. My sister ordered two gin and tonics. We both hated gin, but in some small way, we had to pay for what we had done.

Pink dresses and slippers. Cardigans and beads. Semi circles of nodding, sleepy grandmothers grouped around the television set. Mum got bigger.

'She's eating well,' they said, 'but we haven't the staff to take them outside much.'

Mum and I sitting on a bench on the south cliff, both of us looking out to sea at the sun glinting on the water. Ice cream dripping on her dress. Mum crying quietly. People staring at us. I'd stopped explaining, apologising long ago. She didn't ask for this degrading disease. No one does.

'There's something wrong with me and it makes me frightened.' Her little hand clasped mine. 'Help me, please. Put an end to it all.'

In films someone always seems to say that everything will be all right. It was not all right

One day she couldn't remember who I was. I called to see her on Mother's Day, my arms full of flowers. I smiled at her. She looked away and carried on talking, her words becoming indistinct. Her language distorted.

'Mum, it's me. Hello, how are you?'

Her eyes were dead when they looked at me. She walked out of the room. My throat ached. I sat outside on the low wall and cried tears of disbelief. I rang my husband, not able to make any sense. What can anyone say? The person you once knew is no longer there.

It was then that the visitors stopped coming.

'There's no point.'

They were unanimous in that.

'She doesn't know me. It's a waste of time me coming.' I knew the feeling. I found it hard too. Some loyal friends stayed with her, kept coming, willing her to know them again, searching for the Margaret they once knew.

'She's disturbing other residents,' we were told on Mother's Day a year later. 'She steals their things. She writes her name on everything. We found these notes which she has dropped from her window.' Tiny pieces of paper were handed to me. 'Help me,' they said, in shaky writing.

'We need to give her tranquillisers. She won't sit still. She gets too agitated. We don't have the staff to cope. We've had complaints. Do you think you could find her somewhere else to live?'

We found a little piece of paradise amidst all this, twenty minutes from my home. A circular, glass built unit, full of sunshine, with a garden of lavender and roses, a staff with a sense of humour and lots of love to give.

'Aunty Margaret,' they said, 'you come and stay with us.'

The tight knot inside me loosened, as those once dignified, now bewildered people adopted me. Round the circular route Mum and I would travel, gathering people. Sometimes as many as eight of us would snake in and out of the rooms, hand in hand, gentle and trusting. Talking, constantly talking, in a language as yet unknown to mankind. We would meet Lydia, who would spend her days meticulously examining every cushion in every room, pulling them out and making a barricade for us hikers.

'Who's done this?' Jack, our leader, would come to an abrupt halt. 'I knew they were after us, we'll have to keep on marching.'

Pauline, dressed in Jaeger from head to foot, a retired headmistress, would always be pounding along in the other direction, her shopping bag laden with toiletries, ornaments, toilet rolls, biscuits and cups, odd flowers and other people's slippers and shoes.

'You look lovely, dear,' she would say to me. 'Can you ring my daughter and ask her to come and fetch me?'

I grew to love the place and its characters. It became my second home. I would sit next to Mum, who would perch on the edge of the sofa, ready to take flight at any given moment, dragging me along beside her in a vice-like grip. She would chatter to me constantly, often getting stuck on her favourite word of the day. A word not yet found in the dictionary. The carers would laugh and chatter with the residents and the light-hearted banter would flow.

'It's time you rang my daughter,' Pauline would announce for the tenth time in a minute.

'We will, dear, we will.' They soothed her.

'Ribble, ribble ribble,' my mother would declare.

'Do you think so?' I queried.

Mum would nod solemnly.

'They're coming!' Jack would announce loudly from the doorway.

Joyce would lead him to the trolley and he would look around furtively. Lydia would appear, her arms full of cushions, panting and exhausted.

'Thank you, Lydia,' Carole would call out.

'She's never grateful is she?' Lydia would sip her tea, balanced on cushions, shaking her head. Pauline would then return with all the toilet rolls she could find, stacked high in her handbag.

'They're so heavy!' she would pant. 'Have you rung my daughter, yet?'

'Sod off the lot of you!' Jenny would declare from the corner of the room. 'Is my dinner ready?'

And I would sit, a part of it all, feeling quite at home as they all arrived pink and shining from their baths, ready for a milky drink and a goodnight hug. Sometimes I thought there was more sanity with these people in their own worlds, than the one that I lived in myself.

I got a phone call at work to say that she had had a fall. 'She's in hospital.' I was informed. 'She has to have a hip replacement.'

I arrived at a faceless, concrete block of a building in an area I didn't know. Panic flooded inside me as I tried to find where they'd put her, searching the wilderness of corridors for that one special person. She was in a room all alone, lying on her back, staring at the ceiling. The bed had bars round it. She plucked endlessly at the sheets. I called her name and she turned to look at me, her face wet with tears.

'Mum, it's all right. I'm here. You are in hospital.'
Her face displayed real terror. She clutched my hand and babbled in her own language, her eyes darting wildly around the room. I tried to soothe her but she was obviously in pain. She cried out when I left the room, but I had to find someone, to make them understand.

'She's got Alzheimer's,' I explained to a harassed-looking nurse, 'she doesn't understand what is happening to her.'
That was the problem, she didn't understand. Nobody did.
However, she wouldn't be beaten. She was dancing in a few weeks time, and became Lydia's assistant in collecting cushions.

But things were starting to change. She grew dreadfully thin and then started to lash out at the carers. During our last Christmas together she learnt to hug people again. It was as though she realised she had little time left with us. We had mince pies and sherry and my husband helped her to open her presents. She took my daughter's face between her hands, the little girl she had loved and looked after during those early years.

'You are lovely,' she said distinctly. The first coherent words she had said in many months.

At the Christmas party we danced to "We'll Meet Again," and we both got giggly after drinking too much mulled wine.

When she was dying, she fought to stay with us. The doctor gave her three days, but she was having none of that. I filled the room with bluebells and candles. My daughter sat by her bedside, washed her and talked to her. Roles were reversed. We played her favourite music. I sang to her, James Taylor, You've got a friend. I read to her, excerpts from my father's diaries from the war. I talked to her constantly, 'Do you remember when...?' People who had previously declared that there was no point in visiting her, sat by her bed and cried.

I watched, trying to forgive. We all watched, we three sisters, and waited, trying to fill her last hours with as much love as she gave us. She wouldn't give up. She wasn't ready. We watched her sleeping and then she woke up suddenly, stared straight past us and smiled. She held out her arms. We looked round, expecting to see someone in the doorway. I stood in front of where she was looking and she frowned, and tried to peer around me.

I moved out of the way. My sisters and I held on to each other tightly.

'I think Dad has come for her,' I said.

Once, when I was alone in the room with her, I fell asleep, my head resting on the bed. I woke with a start to see my mother smiling at me. She reached out her hand and clasped mine very gently. 'Hello, my darling,' she said.

She died in my arms, four days before her eightieth birthday. She hadn't woken up for three days, and just before she died, she opened her eyes and looked straight at me.

'Go on, Mum, you can go now,' I whispered, 'Bob will be waiting for you.'

I sat with her for a long time. I remembered the good times. I remembered how she had taught me to love life. How much she had given to me. Unconditional love filled every corner of the room.

Invisible Sun

Is life a drama for all teachers? Do we attract comedy and tragedy in vast amounts?

Are we merely poor players upon this little O? Certainly I always discouraged my own children from ever considering the profession. But has it really been all that bad?

I trained from 1968 to 1971.What a time to be young. The Beatles, Ban the Bomb, Carnaby Street and crocheted hats, mini skirts and mini cars, the Mersey Beat and Mateus Rose. Our career options at the convent were, a nurse, secretary, teacher or in rare cases, university. I wasn't a rare case. Not bright enough. Not rich enough for finishing school. Not enough contacts for a rich husband. Blood and bed pans, no.

So here I was. Flowery Meadows and not a blade of grass in sight. A concrete rabbit warren in the heart of 70s Manchester, with the dank smell of dust, sweat, neglect and unfettered hormones, wax polish, and fear. And the fear was from me, and from the rest of the staff.

Ten staff had resigned and I was filling in between jobs and marriages. A baby daughter, a disappearing husband, and a mortgage made me keep on working.

The staff room teemed with new recruits, their faces like startled rabbits. The old untouchables huddled in groups, finding solace and survival in cynicism, and Players Number 6. The too-large clock, on the wall above the door, clicked its black pointers towards nine o'clock. We inspirers of the young waited, hands clasped around steaming cups of caffeine, eyes darting to the relentless clock, waiting to go over the top into No Man's Land.

The bell. The harshest sound on earth.

'Right' A ferrety looking scientist, all beard and corduroy led us out with a rallying cry, 'Two hours to the bell. Chuck 'em out if they give you grief.'

And that was the discipline policy of the school, poured over in countless staff meetings around the country. A one-sentence document: Chuck 'em out.

I waited in an airless classroom, in sensible shoes and clearly laid out lesson plans.

The door was kicked open. Ten six foot youths belched into the space, finally coming to settle in an amoebic mass, arms flipped over the backs of chairs, boots on the desks. Ten pairs of disillusioned eyes challenged me. Faces were bright with acne, skulls tattooed with MUFC, their boot soles turned towards me in defiance, forming a barrier between us. This was my class. My soon - to - be lovers of Shakespeare and Milton.

'Girls are in the bog,' I was informed.

Then they arrived, all three of them, battered and bruised by the world, at fourteen. Heavily made up faces, dull hair, sad eyes, but mouths that would strip paint off walls.

'An hour in the bog and you're still ugly'

'At least I can do something about it, you'll always be ugly, Gallagher.'

The smallest girl struck, flinging her bag across the room at him, which he dodged neatly with a loud snort of contempt.

Don't let them smell your fear, be confident!

I smiled.'Hello, I'm your new English teacher, Miss Welford. Please sit down, girls.'

I was ignored. Gallagher had been in a fight with his stepfather. They wanted to hear, they desired to be updated. This was a soap opera played out before them, and for my benefit too, I felt. It was generally known that Gallagher's mother was a local lady of dubious morals, and Gallagher was protecting her honour.

'I'm here to teach you, English'

I smiled brightly, determined to win them over.

'He's a hard bastard that Neeley, did you deck 'im?'

'Kicked 'im in the nuts.'e won't be showing me Mam a good time anymore.'

'Now, how many of you have heard of Thomas Hardy?'

There was a silence, as they pondered this. So they were listening, albeit selectively.

'Didn't 'e leave last year? Works in 'is Dad's garage?'

The smallest girl answered helpfully, as she swept past me to sit on Gallagher's desk.

I was losing this round.

'Now, look,' I said, firmly.

There seemed to be some kind of dispute over plans for the evening and I had lost their attention.

'I can't go tonight I 'ave to baby-sit. Our Crystal's just 'ad another kid.' The most scary of the girls, who was called Melody, sat on the desk, combing lots of blond hair, showing rather more thigh than was necessary on a school day.

'Can I have your attention?'

'Will you please listen?'

"Stop talking, now!"

I could hear my voice becoming hysterical. I had no control. Tears darted into my eyes. I was losing it.

I sat down, reached in my bag for my Cosmopolitan magazine, placed my feet up on the desk and started to read. I tried to immerse myself in the air-brushed lives of the famous, whilst mayhem was happening around me. I was a buzzing antenna, every sense alert.

A patch of sunlight drifted through a bullet-like hole in the shattered, grimy glass. Particles of dust danced freely. The bright shaft lit up part of my left hand. The gold on my wedding ring glinted, mocking me.

'Hey, you Teacher!'

I lowered my magazine, and stared into rows of defiant eyes.

'Leave them kids alone,' I smiled as I flipped over a page.'Do you recognise the grammatical error?'

It was lost on them.

'You're supposed to be teaching us!'

Melody's voice crackled over the space between us.

'You're supposed to be listening!' I said to my magazine.

'You should be teaching us!' Her voice almost dissected my eardrums.

I lowered my feet and leant over the desk so that my eyes were level with hers. She didn't flinch and neither did I.

'How?'

'Y'what?' She looked round for support.

My eyes never left her face.

'How exactly am I supposed to teach you when you won't shut your mouth for long enough to hear me.'

A trickle of laughter gave me an indication that my army was gathering, and I wondered fleetingly how many rules in the teacher's handbook I had already broken. She went beet red and opened the cavern for another onslaught, when Gallagher interrupted her with, 'She's right, shut it, Wrightson, let's hear what she has to say.'

I was mildly surprised but kept my cool as the elegant Wrightson spluttered. I stood up and left the security of the desk behind. I faced them. They were quiet. They were listening.

'What bands do you like?' I asked.

They looked at each other.

'I have to teach you poetry,' I explained. My palms were sweating. Could they see how much I was shaking? 'You know, music, groups, bands....?'

'Police' Gallagher's acne - infested side-kick volunteered.

'Police ain't poetry.' A quiet, grubby-looking boy, with the saddest and most beautiful eyes, sat alone, isolated from the rest.

'Song lyrics are the same as poetry,' I explained.

'Young teacher, the classroom, a schoolboy's fantasy.' Gallagher leaned forward.

I had to ignore that one. The water was getting deep.

'Who has any Police records at home?'

A normal question, how naïve I was. How unaware. There was no reply. Nobody volunteered.

'Well, I have,' I lied, wondering if I could catch the record stores before the shops closed. I looked at their blank faces and swept my lesson plans into the bin.

'Poetry by Sting it is.' I smiled. 'Now tell me which ones you like and why.'

The Police saved my life. Sting, I owe you. The words of the songs went up on the blackboard each day. We discussed, we analysed, but there were rules. They would cooperate to an extent if, at the end of each lesson, I allowed the boys to play cards and the girls to chat. Sometimes their armour showed chinks. They were curious.

'Are you married, Miss?'

I hesitated.

'No.'

The boys sat up, interested.

'You've got a child's car seat in your car.'

Ten marks for observation.

'I'm divorced.'

"So's my Mam," volunteered Julie

'Did you dump 'im?'

I wish they'd show as much interest in my lessons.

'No he went off with someone else.'

There was a faint frisson of sympathy.

'"Look can we just get on,' I asked, frustrated by their questions and the noise from the pupils outside, as they were heaved into the corridors. There seemed to be some kind of wheeling and dealing going on right outside my door. I had to investigate.

'What's going on?' I asked as wisps of smoke trailed into the atmosphere, behind innocent looking faces.

A wiry lad who looked as though he hadn't had a square meal for years piped up. 'Can we come in Miss?'

'What do you mean?'

'Gallagher says your lessons are ace and we've just been chucked out of maths.'

I continued to stare.

'It's borin' out 'ere,' whined a pretty girl with a downcast mouth and a chest bursting out of her grey- collared blouse. 'Can we come in and listen to Sting?'

'We don't just listen, we talk about the songs too.'

'I can talk too,' The chest moved forward.

I put my hand across the door, barring their way.

'Fags out and no swearing.' I looked them in the eye.

They trooped in and my classroom filled up. Standing room only.

Peter, with the beautiful eyes stood eagerly by my old Dansette record player.

Nobody would sit near him,'Because he stinks,' Gallagher informed me.

So, Peter put on the record after we had discussed it. It made him feel important, and it was the first time I saw him smile. During the card game at the end of the lesson, he put the record back in its sleeve and closed the lid carefully. He couldn't play cards, they wouldn't let him, and if the mood of the class was hostile, which was often directed towards me, he was also a recipient.

How could I blame them? They carried around more baggage than I could handle. Most of the parents did try their best, but there was poverty and crime and high unemployment. Some of the kids came to me each day from a house of anger and abuse. What did I expect? Maybe they saw me as one of them, divorced and rejected, but according to them I was posh, and I was the authority they kicked against. But they kept coming, until my classroom was crowded and my colleagues were teaching to empty classrooms.

However, no amount of persuasion would make them befriend Peter. I kept him behind after the class has gone. He had no friends waiting for him. I asked about his Mum. He said he hadn't got one. I asked about a washing machine at home. He said they didn't have one. I got the support of the domestic science teacher. We gave him an old P.E. tracksuit. She washed his uniform in her machine. He was on free school meals so at least he got one meal a day.

He lost all his books. The headmaster caned him for not doing his homework. It was my first dispute with the hierarchy. Then he didn't come to school. I was called into the senior mistress's office.

'Peter has been taken into care,' she informed me. 'He won't be coming back. He's been sleeping on his doorstep all this week. His father won't have him in the house anymore. Social services have been round. His father is an alcoholic and can't and won't look after him.'

The class were subdued that day when I walked in. I was angry with them for being insensitive, and angry with myself. Angry at the parents who inadvertently screw up their kids, and then expect us to cope with the damage. I was fond of Peter and I tried to make a difference, but I'd failed him. We all had.

On Wednesday morning the class were in uproar as one of the girls was pregnant. This promoted a round of sex talks we had to deliver. The class were grinning as I struggled with the carrot and the condom. Gallagher offered to show me how it was really done. I was scarlet with embarrassment.

Melody walked up to the desk. 'Miss, we know all this,' she said in an unusually quiet voice, taking the carrot off me and throwing it back in the box. 'What we want to know is how to get out of this place and get a decent job.'

I looked at them all looking back at me. 'Listen and learn.' I made sure that I looked directly into the eyes of each one of them. 'Whatever happens and however difficult it might be for you, work hard and pass your exams.

Education will give you the freedom to choose what you want to do with your life.'

The teacher I replaced returned after maternity leave. The week before, I told my English class. There was no reaction. They had given me hell, but I had a lump in my throat the size of an egg on my last day. I really cared about those kids, but my time with them was up. I walked to my car, not looking back.

Pinned to my windscreen by the wiper, was a large card with a deformed looking cat sitting in a bed of blue roses. They had all signed the card, under the message,

Good Luck Miss and don't let the bastards grind you down.

I won't, kids. I certainly won't. Thanks to you.

Brief Encounters

It was in the middle of a particularly gloomy February that Will and I decided to join a dating agency. Early snowdrops, pushing valiantly through solid earth to emerge triumphant in a burst of white and green, kick-started my plans for new ventures. As I slithered across the solid ground in spiky heels to meet Will in the Frog and Nightgown, I was determined to move forward and a seemingly reluctant Will was coming with me.

Will and I had been friends since we were fledgling teachers. Sitting opposite to each other on our first day, whilst the sun beamed through the windows, I noticed the cowboy boots and he the mahogany hair – a mistake I had to live with for a while. When our new headmaster stood up to address us in an obscene flowery tie and green corduroys our eyes met, our eyebrows lifted and there was an instant understanding and a firm friendship to follow.

'We are born astride a grave,' he greeted me cheerfully as he looked up from his copy of *Waiting for Godot*. I stumbled into the bar, shooting through the door like a billiard ball, as I skidded on an invisible piece of ice. 'You could kill someone with those heels.' He shook his head at me, as he rose from his seat, slapping his book down on the table. 'Sweet white wine? Blue Nun? Leibfraumilch? Dry wine with a dash of sugar?'

I glared at him. Will thought I was a philistine as regards wine. I'm sure I was.

'I've got the information.' I fixed him a bright smile. I laid out the application forms on the table between us. 'I've filled in most of our details.'

We exchanged a glass for a form, and Will perused the document as though it was his recent divorce papers from marriage number two. He sighed and rubbed at his brown curls,

'Are you sure this is a good idea, Sal?' He looked at me with his brown Labrador eyes. He laid the forms down on the table and smoothed them out carefully.

I glanced at him sharply. 'Don't you dare back out now, we agreed!'

He sighed again.

'Stop sighing, we agreed!'

He looked up beseechingly.'Sal.'

'Will, you can't fall asleep on your beanbag every night, dead drunk, with your guitar still attached to you. I've listened to the songs you write, Jeez, you need to meet someone too.'

He smiled as he always did when I was losing it. 'O.K.' He picked up my pen, 'but I think I'll be 5'8 instead of 5'5.'

'Just wear your cowboy boots,' I grunted, stuffing the forms back into the envelope before he changed his mind.

I got my first phone call on a Monday night. Monday night was yoga with my friend, Jean. The hall was full of candles and the swirling wafts of camomile and lavender, as we lay on our sky blue mats, activating our charkas.

'I can't go, I'm scared,' I hissed at my best friend.

'Course you can go.' She glared at me through her legs, as we did the Downward Dog.

'What if he's a pervert or an axe murderer?'
We both collapsed on our mats together.

'Everyone is screened for God's sake. They just want to meet like - minded people instead of prowling round night clubs,' she panted. 'Just go.'
So I did. I had to, because you didn't argue with Jean.

It was a foul night. The wind rattled at the doors of my car, and the rain thrashed against the windscreen. I sat outside the pub, where I was due to meet man number one, at a quarter past eight. I watched the clock in my car tick by, my life tick by. What was I doing here, how did I get here, to this point in my life? Was I so desperate?

I sped round to Will's flat, puffing up the stairs to his pent-house garret on the seamier side of town.

'What?' he hissed through a crack in the door.

'I didn't go in. I got scared.'

'What? '

'I don't know, let me in. I need a drink.'

He opened the door a little wider. Streams of Miles Davies filtered out. He squeezed himself out into the narrow hall, clutching a bottle of wine.'Go away, Sal, I'm entertaining.' He looked anxious.

'What?'

'She's gorgeous. I think I'm in love.'

'Your first one? You didn't say,' I gasped at him. His eyes twinkled. 'Yes, now, just go away.' He pushed me gently.

'But what will I do?' I wailed.

He shoved the wine into my hand. 'Go!' he whispered.

'You're in love? So soon?'

I know Will's past and it was a disaster, eclipsing mine by miles.

'He grinned, 'Yes, but..'

'But what?'

'She's six foot four.'

He slammed the door before I could think of an answer. I knocked as softly as I could. The door opened a crack.

'Your fly's undone,' I whispered.

'Cheers,' he whispered back, as he shut the door.

I drove home slowly, the rain still whipping and lashing at the windscreen of my car.

I drowned my sorrows in Will's wine and a packet of ready-salted, watching Brief Encounter for the twenty second time. 'Oh, Celia,' I sighed. 'How come you had two men, and I can't even find one.'

'Six foot four!?' I challenged Will on the corridor on the way to assembly.

He looked tired but smug and had an unusual spring in his step. 'I knew you shouldn't have altered your height. You'll look ridiculous together.'

He grinned, 'We didn't stand up for long.'

Scores of students were now surging between us.

'But, have you got lots in common?'

He shrugged, 'Not sure yet, but at least she likes red wine.'

He weaved his way between throngs of pupils who were lining up outside the classrooms.

'Bit of a drawback, 'though, she's hooked on Coronation Street, so we had to watch that first…'

This is the man who only watched documentaries and Art House films, and who railed against British Soaps in his sixth form lessons.

We were being separated again by the slow pace of the sixth form. Will became surrounded by languid admirers. 'Your house, dinner on Saturday,' he said. He peered at me between masses of shiny tresses. 'And invite the second one on your list. We'll be there for moral support.'

What? Will was already part of a 'we.'

I rang man number two, during my lunch hour, knowing that he would be at work, and I could do the cowardly thing of leaving a message on his phone. I suggested brightly that we meet at my house for a meal with friends the next day, and gave him directions.

It was Friday night after work, and Will opened the door of his Jaguar and flung a set of books inside. 'We'll be round about 8,' he said. 'We have to watch a couple of back episodes of Corrie first. By the way,' he stuck his head out of the window just before he drove off. 'She's a vegan and a coeliac. Hope it's not a problem, Delia.' He flashed me a grin and purred off into the weekend.

Date number two. A small, slightly built man, with kindly eyes was standing in my hallway. I took the bottle nervously, feeling optimistic about his choice, and opened the door wider.

'Come in, er.. Sally Baxter…….' I held out my hand, wanting more than anything to run upstairs and lock my door against the world.

'Gordon Stuart." He had a soft Scottish accent, his handshake was firm, and his smile friendly and sincere.

Right Sal, you give this your best shot, I told myself. Previously, I had felt confident, until about 7 o'clock, when after concocting a rabbit – food type meal I dashed upstairs to slap on some make up, and I found it, the beginning of the end, an extra fold of skin on my eyelid. I had trouble putting on eye shadow. It didn't look right. I peered into the magnifying mirror, and there it was. It was happening, the slippery slope into wrinkledom. I was doomed.

I scraped back my hair until it hurt, hoping my eyelids would follow, but no deal. To hell with it! I pulled my fringe over my eyes. The Chrissy Hinde look would do until I found a solution.

'Do come through, I'll take your coat.' I flashed him a smile and closed the door.

He looked nice, perhaps we could make a go of it. My heart lifted. He handed me his coat, and then I saw it. A cardigan. He was wearing a cardigan, with leather buttons, just like my dad. I grinned inanely. 'I'll er get you a drink if you just want to er.. I'm just... ' I waved a hand pointlessly in the direction of the lounge. I couldn't take my eyes off it.

'Wine?' My grin widened so much I must have looked like some species of hyena.

'Great.' He turned and walked into the lounge, cardigan and all. I shut the kitchen door and fumbled for my mobile. Waterfall – like sounds drifted through the earpiece.

'Will, he's wearing a cardigan!'

'Sal I'm having a sla...'

'Come over now, he's wearing a cardigan. I can't deal with this. He's like my dad!'

'Trevor wore a cardigan.'

Trevor *never* wore a cardigan.'

He was nice, really, really nice, like an uncle or a friend of my dad's. The computer must have had a bad day, we were mis-matched and we both knew it. He liked chess. He was fifty. I liked rock n roll and I was forty one, still acting and dressing a decade younger.

Conversation over dinner was difficult at first. Will's woman was beautiful, with legs that went on and on, and Will looked completely besotted for the first hour, until she decided to speak. 'Did you watch Coronation Street?' she asked over coffee.

Will's eyebrows disappeared under his curls.

'I'm an Emmerdale man,' smiled Gordon eventually, after a yawning pause. 'My son is one of the assistant directors.'

'Ooohh, that's amazing!' she squeaked.

'No,' he said apologetically. 'Admittedly, it's good he got the work but I hate it. I watch it out of loyalty. I don't like TV, especially soaps, and I only watch foreign films.'

You go Gordon!

'Amelie?' enquired Will, his eyes brightening.

'I prefer, The Very Long Engagement,' replied Gordon stirring his coffee. He looked up at Will.

'Me too,' Will was excited, and then they were off, talking non -stop.

The face of Will's companion was like stone for the rest of the meal, and I became busy with the dishes, trying to occupy myself so I didn't have to talk to anyone. Will and Gordon hardly paused for breath, Will's woman disappeared in a huff, and Gordon and I came to an understanding that although we were not destined for each other, he'd found a soul mate in Will. They retired to the pub for last orders, still talking, and I watched *Brief Encounter* for the twenty third time, after pinning back my eyelids with sellotape.

March arrived and driving rain swept through the corridors of school. The kids arrived to lessons wet and fractious and their uniforms steamed as we ploughed through the Romantics. Daffodils danced and so did Will, as woman number four was into salsa. He was having the time of his life. Then he dropped the bombshell.

A late frost had peppered the landscape and we were out walking the hills, forsaking the pub for a healthier life-style, enjoying together the patchwork of fields below, the sun sparkling on the grass.

'Sal,' he turned to look at me, his cheeks flushed from the cold and eyes watering endearingly with the cold blast from the north east wind, 'I'm getting married. Will you be my best man?'

A dog barked somewhere in the valley below, and my insides were doing somersaults in the silence that followed. 'Can I meet her first?'

'Sure.' He put his arm round me and gave me a kiss.

That night I rang the next man on my list. This would be the last one, then I'd give up. The date lasted half an hour. I excused myself, went to the loo and bolted. I ran.

'What are you running from , Sal?'

I sat on Will's lumpy sofa and downed my glass of Piesporter.

He sat opposite to me and put his hands on my knees so he could look straight at me.

'I don't think you want a relationship at all,' he said. 'You are scared of getting involved, of anyone getting close to you. Don't arrange to meet these guys if you don't want to. Stop putting pressure on yourself. You've been so much happier on your own since you and Jonathan broke up.'

I sighed. Will was right, as ever. I was beginning to calm down.

'Look,' he smiled in his disarming way. 'Susie will be here in ten minutes, then you can meet her. You'll love her, Sal.'

'Well, you'd better do your flies up first,' I said, hurriedly dialling number four's number, ready to apologise. 'Or she'll think we're more than good friends.'

The lovely Susie and I hated each other on sight. She wasn't right for him. She criticised him. She tried to manipulate him, and he was too good natured to see it. He wasn't allowed to be Will. He was my friend, and he went salsa dancing. The doctor of philosophy who read Proust and ran the debating society at University was salsa dancing with a strikingly beautiful girl with the intellectual capacity of an earwig.

'Do come and watch us,' perky little Susie suggested. 'We're really good. We're going to enter competitions.'

'I'll be away that week,' I declared, pulling on my coat and slamming the flat door behind me.

Will clattered down the stairs after me and seized my arm. He had the little boy lost look on his face, confused, unsure. 'Sal, why are you behaving like this? I don't understand you. I'm really happy with Susie. I'm trying new things, having fun.' He wouldn't let go of me. 'Look I'm sorry you didn't find someone special, Sal, but I did.'

'Oh, please,' I snapped, as I wrenched myself away from him. He caught me as I stumbled down the remaining stairs, 'And will you get this bloody carpet fixed!' I yelled.

His arms tightened around me as I tried to regain my balance.

'Will!' A pathetic wail spiralled above us. 'What are you doing, darling?'

'She called you darling!' I turned so swiftly that we almost bumped noses.

'I love her, Sal.'

'Lust my dear boy, lust. She's got a Jennifer Lopez bum and that's done it for you.'

We were inches away from each other. I could feel his breath on my cheek.

'I cannot be a part of this. I cannot be your best man, Will.'

His lips touched mine so briefly, I almost thought I had imagined it. He smiled, then let me go so suddenly, that the atmosphere around me changed and froze.

'So be it.' He turned and walked back up the stairs, and I watched him, my body a lead weight, a terrible sense of loss overwhelming me.

'Goodbye, Will.'

His door closed. The wind chimes rattled against the wood, and then there was silence. The silence stayed with me on the journey home. The night was grey, the street lamps a fuzzy glow. I saw nothing but the tips of my shoes as they clacked on the wet pavement. I heard nothing until the key turned in the lock of my own door. Inside the silence was louder. I switched on lamps and lit candles, and in the soft glow of the dark light, I began a to-do list for the next phase of my life.

-cancel my membership
-see more of my friends
-see more of my sister and try to like her children
-investigate eye surgery
-join a dramatic society
-get back my optimism
-apologise to all the men I had let down
-let Will go

My cheeks were wet, and I didn't know why I was crying. Will's words – what are you running from - kept churning around and I couldn't find peace. What was I so afraid of?

Why couldn't I give the agency a chance, the men I had met, a chance? But it wasn't the agency that was at fault, or anyone else. I knew that. It was me.

'Thought you might want a drink.'

Will stood in the doorway of my kitchen, clutching a brown paper bag. His Humphrey Bogart raincoat had the buttons done up wrongly, as though he had left home in a hurry.

'Don't you ever knock?'

'Not usually.'He grinned at me. 'Didn't fancy dancing tonight.'

'And the lovely Susie, your fiancée?'

He was making hard work of pulling out the cork.

'She's gone with her mother.'

I paused. 'Does she know you are here?'

'Dunno. Probably. Ah, that's done it – I've brought a nice little Chardonnay, a bit upmarket for you, I know, but the times they are a - changing.'

I looked at him, 'Will, you don't drink white wine, what's going on?'

He reached up into my cupboard for two glasses. 'Put Brief Encounter on, Sal, I'll bring the wine.'

Obediently, I slotted the DVD into the machine. I wasn't getting any answers. I would have to wait. He sat down next to me and threw a packet of ready salted into my lap.

'Ah, chilled white wine.' He took a gulp, wrinkled his nose, and flopped back into the depths of my sofa to watch the film. The minutes ticked by. We watched Celia changing her library books in Boots.

'She wants us to dance at the wedding.'

'Who? You and me?'

Will ignored me. Celia entered the refreshment room, little knowing how her life would change.

'Your wedding?'

'Yes. The wedding you won't be best woman for.'

'Ah.'

Will refilled my glass.' You know, I don't think I'm that keen on salsa dancing anymore.'

Trevor turned towards Celia in the refreshment room at Milford Station, his trilby at a jaunty angle. Will drained his glass and refilled it. 'In fact, I'm not sure I know the difference between love and lust.'

Celia and Trevor were meeting for the first time. I loved this bit, how polite they were, how wonderfully English, and how distracted was I.

Will leant forward. 'Now, look at Celia's shoes. They are sensible, trotting -around-town- to- meet-your- lover- type shoes. Not like those stupid things you totter around in, so I always end up carrying you home.'

I looked at him, trying to tear myself away from the passion that was playing out in front of me. 'Will, should you really be here, when you are getting married in a month's time?'

He ignored me again. He often did this. He refilled our glasses. We seemed to be getting through rather more than usual. He threw off his shoes and stretched his legs out across my lap. 'She says I have to give you up, Sal. The friendship is unhealthy.'

'Why, because we eat too many crisps?' I took a gulp of wine and shifted Will's legs around until I was comfortable. We watched the film in companionable silence for a while, although silences never lasted long with Will.

'You remember Gordon?' He stretched out his legs on the sofa, so that, as usual, I became wedged in a corner.

'Gordon who?'

I was watching Trevor and Celia's developing passion.

'Gordon of the cardigan.'

'Well, what about him?'

I took my eyes off the screen as Celia was at home with her husband, pretending that all was well and that she wasn't bored out of her skull with him, even though he was a nice man, such a very nice man.

'He's starting up a theatre company. He's always wanted to'

The last scene was playing. I willed for them to stay together, stirring their cups of tea forever.

'He was thinking of a good starter, a strong play with a small cast.'

'This misery cannot last. I must remember this and try to control myself.'

Oh, Celia, how true that is, but can I? Did you? Will moved his feet and wedged me further in the corner of the sofa.

'Well, I suggested Brief Encounter, provided it's released for amateurs.'

The first tear started to roll as I willed Trevor not to go, not to leave Celia sitting at the table.

'He wondered if you and I would like to read for the lead roles.'

I struggled to find a tissue. 'But I thought that you and Gordon only liked foreign films.'

Will was excited and animated as he always was at the start of a new project. We had promised ourselves we would join an amateur company but it had never happened. Somehow the timing seemed wrong and I wondered briefly what part the lovely Susie would play in all this.

'Brief Encounter's a classic. David Hare is a genius. I suggested something I knew you would be interested in. He thought we would be ideal as we are easy together.'

Will was running out of words, which was a first. Maybe he thought that I wasn't interested.

I blew my nose as Celia gazed at the train track beneath her.

'Sal will you stop that and listen. You know how it ends.'

'I'm listening. I am." I rummaged in my handbag for another tissue. Why was my bag so full of things I didn't need?

'It would be great, don't you think. You and me, Celia and Trev, with or without the sellotape. Say you'll give it a go.'

For some reason, I couldn't stop the tears. He handed me his handkerchief. It was soon soaked. I wasn't even in your league, Celia. I had lost it completely. Will moved up the sofa towards me and put his arms round me, hugging me close to him, as he had done so many times over the years.

'Thanks for coming back to me.' Celia's husband said.

Biography

Jan Hunter is a Yorkshire born writer, who is married with two grown up children. She is a local correspondent for the Darlington and Stockton Times. A member of York Writers, she recently won their first prize for Flash Fiction and the Northern Echo Short Story Competition in 2005. In 2008, she left her job as Head of Drama in a local school to concentrate on researching her first novel, a time- travel mystery, which is set in Castle Howard. For research she went through regressive therapy in order to access her own past lives. My Two Lives has received 5 star awards and has the backing of Castle Howard's owner, the Hon Simon Howard. Her short story collection includes the award winning story of her mother's battle with Alzheimers. The story is used by South Tees Hospital to help families and carers to cope with the disease.

More information can be found on her website www.janhunterauthor and on Facebook and Twitter.